YOU CAN DO IT, YASMIN!

D0061426

written by
SAADIA FARUQI

illustrated by
HATEM ALY

PICTURE WINDOW BOOKS
a capstone imprint

To Mariam for inspiring me, and
Mubashir for helping me find the right
words —S.F.

To my sister, Eman, and her amazing
girls, Jana and Kenzi —H.A.

You Can Do It, Yasmin! is published by Picture Window Books,
an imprint of Capstone.
1710 Roe Crest Drive
North Mankato, Minnesota 56003
www.capstonepub.com

Library of Congress Cataloging-in-Publication Data is available on
the Library of Congress website.
ISBN: 978-1-5158-6091-4 (paperback)

Summary: A collection of four new stories featuring Yasmin! Whether
she's braving the goalie net for the first time on the soccer field, trouble-
shooting a plant problem in the garden with her family, tackling a tricky
writing assignment, or managing a disagreement with her friends, Yasmin
is always thinking outside the box to come up with creative solutions.
Yasmin can do it!

Designer: Lori Bye

Design Elements:
Shutterstock: Art and Fashion, rangsan paidaen

TABLE OF CONTENTS

CHAPTER 1

A New Coach

It was time for gym class. Principal Nguyen had some news.

"Students, we have a new gym teacher," he said. "Please welcome Coach Garcia to our school!"

"Welcome, Coach Garcia!" the students all said together.

Yasmin looked at the new coach. She looked very important with her whistle.

"What are we playing today?" Ali asked, jumping up and down. "Four square? Freeze tag?"

Coach Garcia shook her head. "Soccer!" she announced. She lifted a soccer ball over her head.

Ali cheered. "Hooray! I love soccer!"

Yasmin frowned. She'd watched lots of soccer on TV with Baba. The players kicked and elbowed and fell down a lot. It looked dangerous.

"I've never played soccer before," she said quietly.

Coach Garcia heard her. "I'm here to teach you," she replied. "It's good to try new things."

Yasmin groaned.

CHAPTER 2

Excuses

Coach Garcia explained the rules of the game. Then she showed the students some moves.

She stopped the ball with her feet. "This is called trapping," she said.

She kicked the ball while running. "And this is dribbling!"

"Now it's your turn," Coach Garcia said.

Ali already knew how to play. He kicked the ball as hard as he could into the net.

Yasmin wondered if it hurt his feet to kick like that.

Emma bounced the ball off her knee. That looked like it *really* hurt.

Yasmin stayed near
Coach Garcia. "Can I be the
cheerleader?" she asked. "I can
yell really loudly."

Coach Garcia shook her head.
"Everyone has to play."

Yasmin watched the others
kick and dribble and trap. One
boy tripped and fell.

"Can I be the water girl?" she
asked. "Everyone looks thirsty."

"No, Yasmin."

Coach Garcia blew her whistle loudly and clapped. "Ready for a game?"

She put the students into teams.

"Can I be the referee? I remember all the rules you taught us," Yasmin begged.

Coach Garcia pointed to the net. "You get to be the goalie," she said firmly.

"*Goalie*?" Yasmin asked with a gulp.

She remembered how Ali
had kicked the ball into the
net. Goalie looked like the most
dangerous job of all.

CHAPTER 3

The Goalkeeper

Yasmin stood inside the goal. She wanted to hide.

Ali kicked the ball. Yasmin ducked. The ball went right into the net. Ali's team cheered.

"Goalies can use their hands," Coach Garcia reminded Yasmin.

Soon Ali's team kicked the
ball toward the goal again. This
time Yasmin jumped to catch it.
She missed.

"Goal!" shouted Ali.

Coach Garcia called out,
"Good try, Yasmin!"

Yasmin got ready again.
Soon Ali's ball came right at her
feet. She rushed toward it—and
tripped. But she stopped the ball!

"You did it, Yasmin!" Emma cheered. "You blocked the goal!"

Yasmin got up slowly. "I did?"

Coach Garcia gave her a high five. "Great job, goalie!"

"You're the star of the team, Yasmin!" Emma said. "Can you teach me that move you did?"

"You were just like the pros on TV!" Ali said.

Yasmin grinned and wiped
the sweat off her face.

"It wasn't even that
dangerous," she told them.

Coach Garcia offered her a bottle of water. *"I'll* be the water girl," she said.

Yasmin gulped down the water.

"Thanks, Coach," she said. "Who's ready to play again?"

Spring Is Here

"Spring is my favorite time of the year!" Mama said one day as she looked out the window.

"Why?" asked Yasmin.

Mama pointed to the sky. "The birds are flying about. And everything is green again!"

Baba nodded. "It's the perfect time to plant our garden!"

"Can I help?" Yasmin asked.

"Of course!" Baba said.

Baba and Yasmin went to the garden store. It was full of spring displays. Sunflowers. Roses. Baby trees.

"This is amazing," Yasmin whispered.

Baba bought some vegetable seeds. Carrots, lettuce, tomatoes, and peppers. He also bought soil and a new watering can.

Yasmin saw small pots of flowering plants all in a row.

"Can I please buy a plant, Baba?" Yasmin asked.

"Only if you promise to take care of it," Baba replied. "A plant is a living thing. You must look after it just like a mama would look after a baby."

Yasmin nodded. "I will, I promise."

CHAPTER 2

Planting Seeds

Baba and Yasmin spent the next day in the garden. It was hard work.

Baba dug holes in the soil, and Yasmin dropped seeds into them.

They covered up the holes
with new soil.

Then they watered the area.

"Grow quickly, little seeds,"
Yasmin whispered.

Next Baba helped Yasmin with her flowers. She chose a perfect place near the window. She could look at them whenever she wanted.

"I'm going to water you every day. I'll take care of you, just like a mama and a baba," Yasmin said to her flowers.

The next day Yasmin peeked out the window. Her plants were wilting! The leaves drooped, and the flowers looked sad.

"Oh no," Yasmin cried, rushing outside. "Maybe the plants need water!"

She gave her flowers a drink.

The next day she checked
again. They were still wilting.

"Maybe they weren't thirsty,"
she said. "Maybe they need new
soil."

She asked Baba for another scoop of soil. Then she patted the soil around the plants.

On the third day, the plants were even more wilted. The little flowers were almost gone.

"What is wrong with my plants?" cried Yasmin. "I've been a terrible mama!"

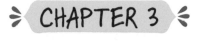

CHAPTER 3

Too Hot

After lunch Nana and Nani came outside to the garden.

"Look at the bright sunshine," Nana said. "I love how it warms my bones."

Nani sat down on a chair and fanned herself.

"The sunshine is making me
too hot!" she complained.

"Yasmin, can you bring your
Nani an umbrella, please?" Baba
asked. "It will give her a little
shade."

Yasmin went inside to the coat closet. She stared at the umbrellas, wondering. It was too hot and sunny for Nani. Was it also too hot and sunny for the flowers?

Yasmin had an idea.

"Here is a big umbrella for Nani," Yasmin said when she got back to the garden.

"Shukriya, Yasmin," Nani replied.

"And a little umbrella for my flowers," Yasmin said.

She put the small umbrella over her plants.

Nana clapped his hands. "Excellent idea, Yasmin jaan!" he said.

Yasmin smiled. "Let's wait and see."

The next day Yasmin and her parents went outside. Her flowers looked happy and healthy.

"Hooray, I'm a good mama after all!" Yasmin said.

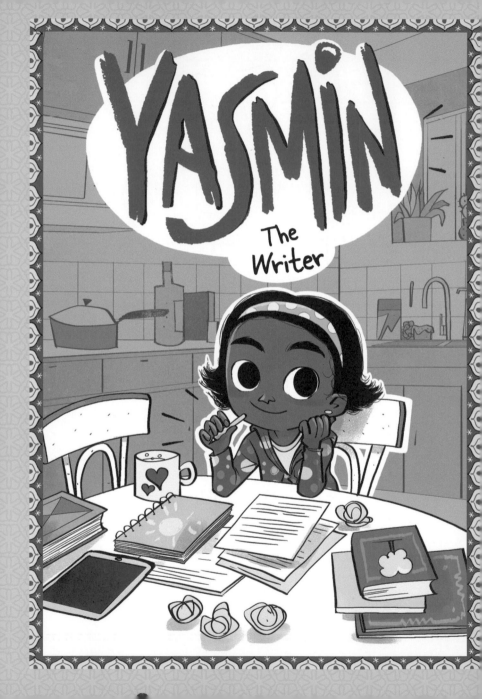

CHAPTER 1

The Assignment

Ms. Alex had a new assignment for the students. "You're each going to write an essay!" she said.

Yasmin raised her hand. "I like writing!" she said. "What will we write about?"

Ms. Alex wrote the topic on the board. **My Hero.** "Does anyone know what a hero is?" she asked.

Emma raised her hand. "Someone who does great things. Someone we can be proud of," she said.

Ms. Alex nodded. "Absolutely!"

Ali was too excited to wait for Ms. Alex to call on him.

"I will write about Muhammad Ali, the boxing champ," he said. "We have the same name. He's my hero!"

"Great choice," Ms. Alex said with a smile.

"I think I'll write about Rosa Parks," Emma said. "She was a brave hero!"

Yasmin tapped her pencil. Who should she write her essay about? She couldn't come up with any heroes.

The bell rang.

"Work on a rough draft tonight," Ms. Alex said. "We'll write our essays tomorrow after lunch."

⇉ CHAPTER 2 ⇇

Thinking Hard

That evening Mama showed Yasmin how to research on the computer while dinner was cooking.

"Here is a list of people who have done amazing things," Mama said.

On the list were a famous
athlete and a music star. There
was a man who donated lots
of money to poor people. There
were queens, presidents, and
other leaders.

But Yasmin shook her head. "None of these are *my* heroes."

"Keep thinking while I finish making dinner," Mama said. "Look, we're having your favorite—keema!"

Yasmin doodled on her paper. "Thanks," she mumbled. Writing an essay wasn't as easy as she'd thought.

The phone rang.

"I got it!" Mama yelled.

Yasmin made a list of ideas.
An explorer? An inventor? A
poet? She sighed and crossed
them out. These were amazing
people. But who was her hero?

"Mama, I can't find my pajamas," Yasmin said at bedtime.

Mama found them in the closet. "Here they are, jaan!"

That night Yasmin had a
bad dream. She woke up scared.
Mama came into her room and
held her close.

"It's okay, my darling," Mama
said softly. "You're safe. I'm
always here."

CHAPTER 3

A Hero to the Rescue

The next morning at school, the students showed their homework. Emma's rough draft had facts about Rosa Parks. Ali had drawn a picture of Muhammad Ali with his boxing gloves.

Yasmin shoved her blank paper into her desk.

At lunch she realized she'd forgotten her lunch box. "Oh no!" she wailed. Her day was getting worse and worse.

Suddenly Mama burst into the cafeteria.

"Yasmin! I'm here!" she panted. She held up Yasmin's lunch box.

"Mama, you're a lifesaver!"
Yasmin said and hugged her.

Mama hugged Yasmin back.
"That's just what mothers do."

Yasmin got an idea. "I guess you could say you're my hero!" After lunch Yasmin knew exactly who to write about.

My hero is my Mama. She juggles many different jobs at home like an expert. She hugs me when I'm worried or sad. She protects me. She saves me from an empty stomach. She is always there. I don't know what I'd do without Mama.

Ms. Alex peeked over Yasmin's shoulder. "Excellent essay, Yasmin! Heroes don't have to be famous people. Sometimes they are the ones closest to us."

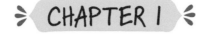

CHAPTER 1

Guests

Yasmin was excited. Ali and Emma were coming over to play.

"I want to have a perfect day," she told Baba. "I will plan lots of fun things to do and yummy snacks to eat."

"Sounds great," Baba agreed. "But don't forget to ask your friends what they would like to do. Friends are a blessing. We should make them happy."

Yasmin brought her box of dress-up clothes into the living room. "We're going to have so much fun!" she sang.

Ali arrived first. He had a bag of small balls with him. "I'm learning to juggle," he said.

"You didn't have to bring your toys," Yasmin said to Ali. "I have lots of things to play with."

Then Emma arrived. She held up a new jump rope. "My uncle gave this to me for my birthday," she said. "Isn't it neat?"

CHAPTER 2

A Fight Between Friends

Yasmin opened her box of costumes. She held up a unicorn suit.

"Let's play dress up," she said. "Nani made these costumes for me. What do you want to wear?"

Ali headed for the backyard. "Nah! I want to juggle. I'm going to be a famous juggler when I grow up."

Yasmin frowned. She and Emma followed Ali outside.

They watched as Ali tossed the balls in the air. One by one they landed on the ground.

One hit him on the nose.

"Ha!" Emma laughed. "You need lots of practice."

She started to jump rope. "Yasmin, count how many times I can jump."

Yasmin shook her head.
"But I want to play dress up,"
she complained.

She didn't
think Ali and
Emma were
being very
good friends.

Ali crossed his arms over his
chest. "I don't want to jump rope
or play dress up. I'd rather juggle."

Yasmin watched as her
friends played by themselves.

Ali juggled by the bushes.

Emma jumped rope. "One,
two, three, four!"

Yasmin groaned. Why didn't
anyone want to play dress up
with her?

A New Game

Baba helped Yasmin make a tray of snacks. There were cookies and gajar to eat. There was mango lassi to drink.

"I'm sure they'll fight over what to eat too," Yasmin grumbled.

Baba patted Yasmin's shoulder. "Remember to think about what your friends want. Not just what you want, jaan."

Yasmin looked out the window at Emma and Ali.

How can I get my friends to play together? Yasmin wondered.

Two squirrels jumped over one another, carrying acorns. Yasmin's eyes grew big.

"I have an idea!" she shouted.

"What's your idea?" Baba
asked.

"You'll see!" Yasmin said and
ran outside.

"Let's play Juggle Jump!"
Yasmin said to Emma and Ali.

Emma stopped jumping.
"How do you play that?"

"We jump rope while juggling balls. We count how many times we can each jump," Yasmin explained.

"Sounds fun," Ali said. "Bonus points if you wear a costume!"

They took turns twirling the
rope and juggling and jumping.
It was so much fun!

Soon they fell down on the grass, laughing.

Baba came outside with the tray.

"Snacks!" the kids cheered. "Thank you!"

"Juggle Jump was a great idea, Yasmin," Ali said while they ate.

"Yes!" Emma agreed. "It's more fun when friends play together!"

Think About It, Talk About It

❊ Yasmin sometimes worries about trying things that are new and scary to her. Think of a time you tried something new. How did you give yourself courage?

❊ Yasmin's family likes to garden together. If you could grow anything you wanted in a garden, what would you grow and why?

❊ Who is your hero? Write three sentences that explain why this person is important to you.

❊ Yasmin's baba says that friends are a blessing. What do you think he means by this?

Learn Urdu with Yasmin!

Yasmin's family speaks both English and Urdu. Urdu is a language from Pakistan. Maybe you already know some Urdu words!

baba (BAH-bah)—father

gajar (GAH-jer)—carrots

hijab (HEE-jahb)—scarf covering the hair

jaan (jahn)—life; a sweet nickname for a loved one

kameez (kuh-MEEZ)—a long tunic or shirt

keema (KEE-mah)—a ground meat dish

lassi (LAH-see)—a yogurt drink

mama (MAH-mah)—mother

nana (NAH-nah)—grandfather on mother's side

nani (NAH-nee)—grandmother on mother's side

shukriya (shuh-KREE-yuh)—thank you

Pakistan Fun Facts

Yasmin and her family are proud of their Pakistani culture. Yasmin loves to share facts about Pakistan!

Islamabad

PAKISTAN

Location

Pakistan is on the continent of Asia, with India on one side and Afghanistan on the other.

(Salaam means Peace)

Language

The national language of Pakistan is Urdu, but English and several other languages are also spoken there.

The word Pakistan means "land of the pure" in Urdu and Persian.

Population

Pakistan's population is more than 200,000,000 people. It is the world's sixth-most-populous country.

Make Your Own Writing Journal

SUPPLIES:

- cereal box or other thin cardboard
- scissors
- about 10 sheets of paper
- hole punch
- yarn
- markers

STEPS:

1. Cut a rectangular piece of cardboard twice as big as you'd like your journal to be.

2. Hold the shorter sides of the rectangle and fold it in half. If the cardboard has a picture you don't want to show, fold so that the plain side faces out.

3. Cut the papers so they're just a bit smaller than the cardboard covers. Stack the papers inside the cardboard like the pages of a book.

4. Along the cardboard fold, use the hole punch to make two punches, evenly spaced. Make sure you punch down through the papers too.

5. Thread a piece of yarn through each hole and tie a knot to hold your pages in place.

6. Draw a design on the front of your journal!

About the Author

Saadia Faruqi is a Pakistani American writer, interfaith activist, and cultural sensitivity trainer previously profiled in *O Magazine*. She is author of the adult short-story collection, *Brick Walls: Tales of Hope & Courage from Pakistan*. Her essays have been published in *Huffington Post*, *Upworthy*, and *NBC Asian America*. She resides in Houston, Texas, with her husband and children.

About the Illustrator

Hatem Aly is an Egyptian-born illustrator whose work has been featured in multiple publications worldwide. He currently lives in beautiful New Brunswick, Canada, with his wife, son, and more pets than people. When he is not dipping cookies in a cup of tea or staring at blank pieces of paper, he is usually drawing books. One of the books he illustrated is *The Inquisitor's Tale* by Adam Gidwitz, which won a Newbery Honor and other awards, despite Hatem's drawings of a farting dragon, a two-headed cat, and stinky cheese.